# *Short Stories*

### *by*

## *Winifred and Norman Barnett*

Highgate Publications (Beverley) Ltd
1994

British Library Cataloguing in Publication Data available

© Executor of Estate of Winifred and Norman Barnett

ISBN 0 948929 85 5

Published by
Highgate Publications (Beverley) Ltd.
24 Wylies Road, Beverley, HU17 7AP
Telephone (0482) 866826

Produced by

4 Newbegin, Lairgate, Beverley, HU17 8EG
Telephone (0482) 886017

# Contents

## Winifred's Stories

## Norman's Stories

# Winifred

## Solitaire

With gentle dignity she glided along behind her lord; queen of the lake; knowing only one master.

No matter that it was only a small lake. In their little world they reigned supreme. No matter that no other members of their species dwelt there: supreme rulers of the lake they were, and had been these many years. The ducks and the water-fowl didn't count, except to do obeisance to their majesty. Imperturbable and invincible; or so it seemed.

People fed them from the bank, exclaiming at their grace, and the sinuous strength of their necks; retreating suddenly and fearfully if a neck reached curiously in their direction. If Penny or her lord paraded the full magnificence of outstretched wings, no one knew whether to leap for safety or to stay and admire the perfection of poise, or the fantastic flight to the farther side of the lake.

Imperturbable and invincible; until, one day, a great clamour brought all the villagers down to the lake-side. There, a battle was raging such as had never broken the peace of that little corner of England for many a year.

A strange cob had just flown in with his mate. He had decided that this should be his territory. Here, where the lake lay like a secret among the trees, he would install his mate. Here, where the bushes bordering the lake, promised such excellent shelter, they would rear a family.

Horrified spectators gazed helplessly as the two males fought for possession; feathers flew, and floated untidily on the water like leaves in a storm. Penny kept her distance, but her serenity belied the fire in her eye.

To the death they fought. But the vanquished lord's dying anguish was hidden from view by the bushes that had been his royal chamber for so many years.

Penny's distress was pitiful. She hurled herself at the usurper's mate in a frenzy of stabbing and tearing, and onlookers transferred their attention to the new battle. But, then, the victorious one left his victim and came back to rescue his mate, and Penny, too, was dispatched to the bushes, battered and bleeding. She did not die, but from then on, for her, 'the king was dead and she was queen'.

When at last she glided out from the bushes on to the lake, they left her alone, and she ignored them.

Time passed, and, in the early summer, a trio of dun-coloured, woolly cygnets emerged from shelter, and swam joyfully out onto the sunsplashed pond. Swifts dived in curving flight throughout the pleasant afternoons; water-hens chuckled gaily, and ducks streaked across the water, competing for the tit-bits that were flung to the swans.

Penny kept to herself . . . a solitary thing, inciting pity, but proudly denying it.

The proud parents swam among their drab offspring, anxious for their welfare; plucking at the loosening down as if to hasten the time when they would be resplendent in shining white feathers. The young cob seemed to come in for more attention than his sisters. It was as if he didn't quite come up to expectations. They were a trifle bigger, perhaps, that was all; but soon they began to pluck him as well: he had no peace. He seemed to be in continuous disfavour with his family.

So that was how he came to attach himself to Penny. Quietly he would follow where she went, scarcely disturbing the clarity of her reflection as she moved along. She gave him no encouragement, neither did she rebuff him, and, quite obviously, he adored her. She was a magnet to him, and soon he was known only as Penny's Chick.

So he grew in peace and achieved his feathers and was a swan.

Winter came, and ended wetly in deluge after deluge that swelled the ponds and the rivers everywhere. The little lake crept out of the old familiar boundaries, and crossed the road, and swept away into the surrounding countryside.

Eventually, however, the rain ceased; and one night, while a large placid moon gazed down on a watery world, Cobber swam out from amongst the waterlogged bushes to where the slender rushes swayed gently with the movement of the water. The water hens wittered softly; they too were restless; and then across the moon-silvered lake he saw Penny. She was unbelievably beautiful. Yet across the distance he sensed a sadness. She seemed to be saying 'Farewell . . . Farewell', as she bowed low over the liquid silver that lapped softly round her. To the young cob she had never seemed so gracious.

Had she forgotten him?

What should he do?

Even as he hesitated, she turned and came sweeping towards him. She had known he was there. Perhaps in the stillness she had caught the sound of his restless feet unconsciously beating the water. When quite close, she stopped, and laid her dripping beak gently in the hollow between his wings. There it rested for a moment; then she floated away into the night . . . alone.

But when morning came, the young cob was once more only a few lengths behind. Penny accepted his presence; and, as the sun rose, a pink ball through the mist, they paddled out of the shadow of overhanging trees into a waste of flooded fields. Everywhere the long grasses speared the surface untidily; the fences waded waist deep, and hedge sparrows chattered anxiously on the thorn bushes.

Penny led the way through a bridge, bending low to avoid the damp and slime that had gathered under the old brick arch. A little further on they reached a farmhouse, its yards and stock awash in the unusual floods. Here they were greeted with shouts of glad surprise, as children from the farm splashed alongside, laughing and throwing crusts to the unexpected guests that the flood had brought them. The swans were not hungry. There was plenty of food in the mud under the water, and they toyed indifferently with the dry bits, poking them under the water disdainfully. Not so the ducks; they clamoured round noisily, snatching at the bits that floated soggily about, and diving comically, to the great amusement of the children.

Day followed day, and the floods settled. The fields grew green again and the little bridge stood high above the water line; and Penny and Cobber stayed on.

At last, when a lazy trickle was all that was left in the bed of the stream, Penny decided that they must go. To stay would be to starve.

The children still came to feed them, but the daily ration was not enough. The ducks were competent scavengers as they poked about in the mud, and Penny forfeited much dignity competing with the ducks for a meagre existence. Cobber was losing weight. He must go.

So, one morning, Penny spread her wings, and sallied incongruously down the tiny creek. Flapping vigorously she heaved herself heavily up, until she rose into the air and over the little bridge . . . and Cobber followed; and the road that lay across the bridge went on its way to London, and the children went back to their play, and the ducks went through into the farmyard to shout rudely at the inhabitants.

But, scarcely had things settled down again than Penny returned.

The children ran out, and stood staring: the ducks came back, wildly curious, as the solitary one clambered slowly over the big stones that were strewn around.

They explained her return thus: she was old, too old to fly far; she had been deserted; perhaps beaten off. And Penny kept her secret. The trailing wing recovered quickly . . . and Cobber had his own game to play.

People fed her well, so well indeed that she grew drowsy. Even when they packed her up and posted her to paradise she relaxed in the comfortable darkness and dreamed . . .

Penny never knew when the dream ended either, for when the drowsiness had cleared the sky was blue above her, and adrift with clouds. There was the soft lap-lap of water quite close, and the smell of wet grass all around. A wide, wonderful lake gleamed near, and, from all parts, dozens of glorious creatures were sweeping towards her.

This, then, was her kingdom.

Confidently she crossed the verdant strip that separated her from her subjects, slid into the water and glided to her place at its centre.

# A Spring Song

He sat amongst the twisted twigs of the old apple tree and practised. His voice was rusty, for, what with the heat and the clouds of dust that he had to contend with during the summer, he had grown lazy, and he had been content to twitter.

His plumage was dull and shabby, and, as for his beak, it was scarcely noticeable; and now it was almost Spring, and he wanted to sing . . . and he couldn't.

One day, as he was flying from the apple tree to the pear tree at the bottom of the garden, he had seen the most beautiful little lady in the world, and he had wanted to be the most beautiful blackbird in all the world in her eyes. He had wanted to sing her the most beautiful love song . . . and he couldn't.

He had felt a most inferior bird.

He hadn't dared show himself. She would not have looked at him favourably; indeed, he feared she would not have looked at him at all.

Just listen to the robin, the bold creature, singing as if he owned the whole orchard. There he sat on the very highest bough of the cherry tree, plainly showing off, and making quite a spectacle of himself. Certainly he was a very elegant fellow in his gay scarlet plumage with the white touches. Up there, against the blue of the sky, the colours were strikingly vivid, and his song bubbled away over the tree tops as clear as the crystal spring.

He, the blackbird, would sing. He would show the whole world how he could sing. He would sing . . . oh, how he would sing . . . for her.

But he was thirsty, his throat felt parched. He would sing much better when he had had a drink from the rain-water butt at the corner of the greenhouse.

The robin was still singing; the wonder was that he did not burst as he swelled his chest and poured out such a flood of silvery notes.

A woman was standing with her feet amongst the violets where they spread a blue carpet all round, even under the bare, prickly gooseberry bushes. She was shading her eyes and gazing up at the robin, delightedly, listening to his rapturous song. She had forgotten that her vegetable basket was still empty, and that the kitchen clock was ticking away the minutes to dinner-time.

He must sing . . . now. And he sang: but his voice mocked him. The notes rasped and grated in his throat.

Nevertheless he persevered. Day by day he practised in the shelter of the old apple tree, and drank the soft rain water, and breathed the sweet dust-free air.

At last, one day, as he was leaning to sip the cool water he saw himself reflected in the surface, and he saw that he was quite black again; his feathers were sleek and shining . . . and his beak, why, his beak was most becoming, it was as gold as the crocuses in the black earth.

Where was the demure little lady of the thorn hedge now?

He would fly round the orchard and look for her. Once or twice he had come upon her sitting on the palings along the side of the garden, but she was very shy. If any one approached she would fly away into the hedge; then he lost sight of her gentle brown form amongst the shadows.

Why, there she was now. She was looking the other way, but she may have seen him. She was much too ladylike to stare.

Very softly, he tried out a few notes of the song that he had been practising: why, it sounded quite sweet.

He would sing a little louder so that she might hear.

Oh dear, now he had frightened her away; what a timid little thing she was. It wouldn't do to make her nervous.

Just the same he kept watch on the gap in the hedge where she had disappeared, and soon he caught the flash of a bright eye as she blinked. He would never have seen her but for that.

She was watching him.

Thus encouraged he flew off to the gnarled old pear tree that was already beginning to shake out the frills of her new spring gown.

He felt wonderful. Suddenly he was singing. Gone were the rasping, croaking notes. He was singing with all his heart now and the melody was sweet and tender. He was pouring out all the beautiful thoughts that were in his heart; the blue sky, the fluffy white clouds, the warmth of the sunshine, the sweetness of the air, the lightheartedness of the breezes, the golden gaiety of the daffodils . . . and the demure charm of his little lady love; and it seemed as if the whole world stopped to listen.

In the hush that followed he heard her answering cry. Then, he was so full of joy that his throat ached to sing again, to release the fountain of song that would tell her of his love.

From below where she sat, discreetly hidden amongst a maze of twigs and branches, she gazed up at him, and her pride in him was tremendous.

What a wonderful creature he was! She was astonished that he thought her worthy of his attention. Why, *she* was such a dull, insignificant bird. Meekly she looked down at her own dim brown feathers and sighed.

Look at his shining black coat; his proud carriage. Look at his brilliant yellow beak. Listen to the liquid notes of his voice.

Yes, she was listening. She had been listening all the time, even when she had pretended to be hunting for worms on the wet grass. She quivered with joy, and stole a little nearer; tenderly yet half fearfully answering his call. Suddenly he was by her side. Then panic filled her, and away she flew, leaping from branch to branch from tree to tree; but always he followed, scarcely a shadow behind, until at last they came to rest in the old apple tree.

There they perched, side by side, swaying gently on the crickly black twigs that were already rosy tipped with promise of blossom. A slit in the old trunk led into the dim heart of the tree; a doorway, perhaps, and soon there would be a sheltering porch of pink and white apple-blossom . . . 'Just the very place to make our home,' sang the blackbird to his mate.

# The Little 'un

'Jim . . meee'! His mother sounded vexed. He lowered the heavy basket to the floor, and the eggs heaved ominously, then settled into place again. 'Leave things like that to Jack. He's bigger than you. You know you can't manage to lift such things,' she grumbled.

It had always been like that: leave it to Jack, he's bigger than you, he's stronger, but Jack was two years younger, too, and that rankled.

Jim scowled and went over to the big table, picking up the newspaper as he went. Spreading out the back page, he scanned the columns eagerly, occasionally referring to a slip of paper which he held. His father, a burly farmer, clumped into the back kitchen. They could hear his heavy tread on the stone flags as he moved about. He would be in soon. *He* would want the paper. Jim's finger slid about rather vaguely, searching . . . searching.

'Got it,' he breathed at last, and then he went slowly through his list, his forehead creasing at his unusual occupation.

'What now, Jimmy lad,' cried Jack in his bantering manner, coming up from behind and peering over his shoulder, 'reading, is it? Horse racing, eh? You thinking of entering our Dolly for the Gold Cup?' he joked.

'Pooh, Dolly's too old for a *Tin* Cup, and you know it. But I would love to see the Gold Cup. Silvergild's a certainty,' said Jim, and began drumming on the wooden table, thrumpetty – tum, thrumpetty – tum, louder, louder, with the rhythm of galloping hooves in his finger-tips.

'Who told you about Silvergild? Shut up making that row. Who told you?' demanded Jack.

'Mr. Martin – gardener up at the big house,' said Jim. 'I've asked him for a job up there. It would only be gardening, but I'd get a look in at the stables sometimes – might even be allowed to help with the horses now and again. I'd like that, if father will agree.'

Father came in soon and made no objections to Jim's idea.

'Go and see the squire tomorrow, lad. I don't think we'll ever make a farmer of you. I dunno how you cum to be such a little 'un, I'm sure.'

'If he'd been bright at school we might have made a black-coat of him, but lesson-books didn't suit him – all he wanted to do was play about with horses, wasting his time, and now he can't . . .'

'Oh, let him alone,' broke in Jack as their mother began working up to a regular tirade. 'He'll maybe make a gardener, given a chance.'

So when Jim disappeared soon after breakfast next morning, nobody bothered. They assumed he had gone up to the big house; and so he had. And almost immediately he was on the road to Newtown in the company of a golden chestnut two-year-old filly that was going for its first race.

Watching the preparations from a short distance away earlier on he had had an overpowering impulse to go and see the Gold Cup Race at Newtown, and here was an opportunity. So, without further ado, he had climbed in and the doors were barred behind him. What would happen if he were discovered he daren't think.

Silvergild was nervous, but Jimmy's gentle murmurs seemed to soothe her. The firm strokes of his hand on her glossy neck brought a soft questing nose round to his face searching for comfort. He rubbed her long nose, caressed her ears and did all those little things that Dolly loved so much. Then he heard them climbing into the cab, the driver and Old Ben the stable boy. He pressed himself flat against the partition, as the sliding panel opened and Ben looked through to see how Silvergild was settling.

Jim spent most of the journey sitting on the floor, his shiny leather leggings and his boots hidden by the loose straw; and the chestnut made no more fuss.

It was a long way to Newtown from Kelsey, more than a hundred miles, so when at last they entered the town he was feeling hungry. He hadn't wanted much breakfast, but he had made himself some bacon sandwiches. They were in his pocket now, and he patted the bulge on his hip; but he didn't eat them straight away – he'd be hungrier still later on he guessed. He couldn't see through the high, tiny windows but he used his ears to good purpose, and it was easy to tell when they were running through the town. When they stopped he hoped that in the excitement of getting Silvergild out he would be unnoticed. Fortune favoured him in this respect. The filly was difficult, and Old Ben had to concentrate all his attention on leading her carefully down the ramp. But then fortune turned difficult too, and Jimmy found himself an unwilling prisoner – bolted in from the outside. He squirmed. He had to get out somehow. He must. But worse followed. The driver shouted something indistinguishable to Old Ben, started up the engine, and drove off, while Jim nearly hammered on the partition in his disappointment. What if they drove right out of the town again? What if he couldn't get back to the races after all? Oh – oh – oh!

But it was only a short ride, after all. They bumped and rattled over a rough patch of ground, then stopped, turned and backed, and Jim realised with relief that the horse-box was now parked. There was a muffled thud as the driver dropped to the grass, followed by the crash of the cab door, and Jim felt oddly deserted. However, now was his chance to scramble about without attracting attention. He must get out. He rattled the doors in a forlorn hope of dislodging the bars, but they held – no hope there. He prowled about, kicking at the straw; no hope of climbing through the windows either, too high and too small . . . unless . . . *could* he get through the panel into the cab? Why not? They were always telling him he was 'a little 'un'.

He pressed the panel open, then tried to hoist himself up high enough to get his head through, but his leather boots wouldn't grip the smooth wood, and he slid down, ramming his chin badly on the framework. He rubbed it ruefully with his cap as he gazed round his little prison.

Suddenly he knew what to do. He rolled up the horse blankets as tightly as possible. They made an unsteady perch, but at any rate they supplied those extra inches he needed, and it wasn't long before he had his head and shoulders through the panel, and by dint of much wriggling and twisting the rest of him followed and he slipped down on to the seat in a heap. He laughed aloud excitedly.

It was a good thing nobody was near enough to see his performance for he had quite forgotten Old Ben and the driver and everyone else while he had been worming his way through.

The rest was easy. Down he jumped on to the grass and pushed the door shut after him, and he was free. He'd made it.

He could see the race course not far away across the grass, but, my, what a busy road! It was streaming with cars, more cars than Jim had ever dreamed of. How would he ever get across? He felt scared. All those people: why, they were flocking up the slope like sheep with all the sheep dogs in Kelsey after them.

He dawdled about on the grass a bit, getting his bearings. Hunger started gnawing again, so he pulled out his flattened, uninteresting paper packet and ate squashed bacon sandwiches with great gusto. That felt better . . . oh, he'd get across that road somehow. And he did.

He found the gate where the horses and jockeys went in, and he found several other gates, but, goodness, he'd never thought it would cost so much to go in. He hadn't enough money . . . and that was that.

When people had paid and gone in he was still leaning against the gate-post, like a disappointed child.

'You coming in or not?' asked the gate-man, 'It's only a quarter of an hour to the first race.'

'No,' said, Jim, rather uncivilly because of his disappointment.

But the man, sensing a minor tragedy, went on, 'You lost your money or something?'

'No,' said Jim shortly, 'haven't enough though.'

'Well, now, you go to that far gate; go past those buses,' he pointed helpfully, 'and you'll see quite a bit from there. The horses all come round that bend.'

Jim's face brightened. 'Oh, thanks,' he cried, and ran off.

It seemed a long way from all the crowds and the noise and the excitement, but there were two or three other people there, so he waited hopefully.

They could hear the loudspeaker, though, and when it blared loudly 'They're off' his hands clenched excitedly, though he couldn't see anything for a while. It seemed an age before his ears caught the drumming of the hooves on the turf; and then the horses hurtled round the bend, almost leaning on the white rails . . . and then they were gone. It was over in a flash. He heard the roar of the crowds rise to a crescendo, as, somewhere out of sight, one of those flying figures passed the winning post.

He waited impatiently for the second race, and then the third, chafing against the delay. He talked a bit to a small boy who seemed to be sucking endless lollipops. His mother said she always brought little Timothy to see the horses, but Timothy didn't really seem very interested, he was much more interested in his lollipop.

'Look, Timothy, look, quick, or you'll miss them.'

'Mmmmm . . .' was all that emerged from Timothy's sticky little mouth as his eyes followed the swift passage of the horses. 'Can I have an ice cream now, Mummy?'

'Oh, all right, come on quick before they come round again,' and Timothy was hauled away at a trot.

After they had moved away, a policeman said to Jimmy, 'You could go as far as those next railings, if you like; you'll see more from there. Don't go any further though.'

Jim was very grateful and when the fourth race went by he was very thrilled indeed. There was only a narrow strip of grass between him and the horses and he really could see much further up the course. He turned and waved to the policeman.

Timothy was back – engrossed in his ice cream.

Once again Jim heard the loudspeaker giving last minute details. 'They're lining up . . . they're under Starter's Orders' . . . and then . . . 'they're off' came the ringing shout. And this was Silvergild's race. She would be running this time. Would she win? Oh, he did hope so. Perhaps he would be able to hear the loudspeaker above the din if he listened hard.

He climbed onto the top rail, tense, waiting for the throbbing that seemed to begin inside him before he really heard it. The dull pounding of many hooves was hammering in his ears as the first horse hurtled round the bend. Then it happened – with sickening suddenness: a mass of straining, stretching bodies, ears laid back, eyes wild, tails a-flying, streamed into view; one heaved itself out of the mass, its speed too much for the curve. In terror it leaped at the dividing rails, throwing its rider as it landed clumsily in the strip between the course and where Jim stood transfixed.

Screams from behind pulled him back to reality. Timothy was back there. The frantic horse was tearing towards him. In a matter of seconds it would reach the very rail where he was standing. He freed his heels instinctively. He didn't think – no time for fear – he just waited while three seconds hammered slowly into his brain, thump . . . thump . . . thump. Then he sprang, just as the chestnut body crashed over the fence.

Somehow it regained its balance, somehow Jimmy's thin arms clung round its neck, and he was swinging crazily alongside – towards a petrified child with an ice cream halfway to his gaping mouth. He knew he must pull that poor terrified creature round, round . . . away . . . from . . . him.

Desperately he clung till the pace slackened, and his boots bumped jerkily on the turf. And then she stopped, bewildered and trembling. Jim's arms stayed comfortingly round her neck. Indeed, he didn't know if he could have unwound them for a few minutes. He leaned his forehead against the pulsing neck and so they stood, each glad of the contact. It was quiet here. They had left the unnerving shouts well behind. But they would have to go back. Someone would be coming to fetch her. His legs felt weak and clumsy as he turned Silvergild round and walked along beside her.

A group of people were approaching now, and he gripped the lead a little tighter. He could recognise the policeman and Old Ben and the jockey, who was apparently very little the worse for his fall.

The admiration, the thanks, the limelight simply confused Jimmy; his ears burned with embarrassment, so, taking advantage of his smallness, he ducked under the boundary rail and made for an open gate. Once outside he crossed the main road that would soon be teeming with traffic again.

He would wait near the horse boxes. He might be able to slip in and travel home with Silvergild again. Poor Silvergild! Jim felt sure she had recognised him.

It wasn't long before he saw them coming, Old Ben and Silvergild. They were getting nearer and he was hoping that they had not seen him when a shrill voice near at hand cried, 'Look, Mummy, there's that boy that stopped the horse. Wasn't he brave?'

Jim's face flamed. Old Ben had heard, too. It was no good hiding now. He might as well go out to meet them.

It seemed natural that Old Ben should hand the reins to Jim while he lowered the ramp and made ready for the return journey. It seemed natural that Old Ben should offer him a lift when he said he must get back to Kelsey that night, and he accepted thankfully. But he was rather nonplussed when Old Ben said, as he was busy turning up the ramp and bolting the doors, 'Aye, well, you'd better ride in front this time, mi lad.' And there was a knowing gleam in his eye as he handed Jim his old cloth cap.

Jim picked the pieces of telltale straw out of his cap and pulled it well down on to his ears – and grinned – and forgot that he was only 'a little 'un'.

9

# Miss Cherry

She came regularly, wet or fine. Sometimes in the morning with the first flow of feet towards the city; sometimes in the early evening, when the colours were accentuated by artificial light. She would stand and gaze at the glory of the flowers in the shop window, drinking in the sweetness of the violets and the gaiety of the anemones, sheltered by a canopy of mimosa.

The little bunch of stuffed cherries would roll about the brim of her old greenish-black straw hat, as she lifted and lowered and turned her head.

How she loved the flowers . . . but she never came in to buy.

One day, a man's voice peered closely over her shoulder and a teasing voice said, 'No use, Mary Ellen, them's not for the like of you an' me.'

'They make no charge for lookin', Sam,' she rapped back, with a bright smile, 'And this 'ere bit of pavement's public property too.'

She held a brown paper carrier bag in an un-gloved hand, and her shoes looked all too thin for damp pavements. There could be no doubt that her income was as inadequate as her shoes. Her only extravagance was time. This for a while would seem to be of no importance; then she would turn quickly, and patter away like a busy little alarm clock trying to catch up with the rest of the day.

It had been a dull day; clouds hung low. People slopped and splashed their way through the pools. The shop-keepers had lit their lamps early. Afternoon shoppers, their baskets heavy with groceries, their brows furrowed with gloom, dutifully bade one another, 'Good afternoon.' But the flower shop window held magic for most of them; they couldn't help smiling a little at its profusion of colours.

Just as Sam moved off into the crowd, a car stopped at the kerb side. From inside the shop, Mamie saw it arrive as she looked through a gap in the lattice and across the wealth of flowers. She turned, and prepared to greet her customer . . . a customer of some importance, if one could judge by such things as furs and shoes and jewels. She had avoided the puddles carefully on her way from the car to the open shop door.

Once inside, her glance took in the blooms with the eye of a connoisseur . . . 'Today I will have pink and white — pink tulips and white lilac,' she said.

Mamie gathered the flowers together, long stalks dripping and cool, wrapped them in the soft folds of tissue paper and handed them to the fur coat. The proud pink tulips leaned luxuriantly against the fur and breathed the soft perfume of the early lilac; the bracelets jangled as my lady sought her coins.

The little bunch of cherries was quite still; the face under the brim of the hat watched the little tableau eagerly. She was still watching as, half smiling, my lady once again stepped daintily between the puddles. Then there was a gentle 'flop' — and one proud, pink bloom lay on the pavement.

Boots and shoes and pram-wheels stamped and churned dangerously near. At any moment it would be ground into a pulp. And she, the proud one, didn't even notice its loss.

There was a slam as a car door closed — a purr as the car moved away. A hand reached towards the flower and almost grasped it; but a sudden movement behind her sent Miss Cheery sprawling beside the flower she had tried so hard to rescue.

People crowded round. Some shouted advice; some tried to help; and some just started and got in the way. Mamie was among the first there. She had already picked up the old slippers and grubby apron, thrusting them back into the privacy of the carrier bag, when a policeman crossed the street and took charge.

'You should clean up such as this, Miss. It's dangerous. Makes the flags slippery,' rebuked the Constable, scraping the remains of the fallen blossom into the gutter with the toe of his shoe.

'I'll be alright in a minute — let me be — I didn't slip on anything,' Miss Cherry protested, understanding Mamie's hurt look. 'Twas my own fault' young man.'

She started, as a gruff voice beside her said, 'Come on Mary Ellen, I'll see yer safely 'ome.' Over his shoulder to Mamie he added, 'thanks Miss; she'll be a'right with me.'

Mamie watched them go, glad that Sam was there, seeing a genuine kindliness in the way he supported her, one big hand cupped under her elbow. He leaned across and chivalrously took the carrier bag in his other hand as they went slowly on their way.

Minutes later, Mamie was back behind her counter serving customers. Along with their requests for posies of this and bunches of that came the questions:

'Has someone been knocked down?'

'Was she hurt?'

'Who was she?'

Mamie didn't know. Come to think of it, she knew very little about Miss Cherry — and less about Sam.

Still, as the days passed and Miss Cherry didn't come to see the flowers, Mamie grew anxious. She looked through the trellis, across the massed heads of tulips and between the sprays of mimosa, to the faces that looked in through the window. All kinds of faces came and went — young faces, glowing like the blossoms, perhaps dreaming of wedding bouquets; old faces kindled to brightness with memories of yesterday; the snub noses of children leaving smeary marks on the glass where they'd pressed against it.

But no Miss Cherry . . .

How Mamie missed her lined old face and the wonder that shone from it. And what a long time it seemed since that lone pink tulip fell from the arm of luxury.

# Skates

From his bed Billie watched the other children playing around the ward, and suddenly a big plastic hoop bowled down the aisle that separated the beds from the centre tables and the large square stove-blocks. When it reached the foot of his bed, it swung gracefully round . . . and the next moment he had caught it in his outstretched hand.

It was smooth to touch.

It was shiny and red.

And he loved it.

One day he would have one, and he would run alongside it all the way along the promenade at the seaside – together they would go faster than the wind.

'Give it to me, Billie; it's no good to you. I'll send it right up to your bed again soon, and I'll race it – you watch.' And with that the hoop was snatched from his hand.

Billie didn't answer. The magic had gone. His head dropped back heavily on the heaped pillows. As he had held the hoop, he had felt himself tingling with anticipation, but . . .

'Oh, bother . . . bother!' he burst out, looking fiercely at the unoffending whiteness of the ceiling.

'Billie Benson, what's a bother?'

And turning his head sideways Billy frowned at a square of starched white apron.

'Oh, Nurse, red's such a beautiful colour.' And he waved his hands reflectively over the white bedcover.

'Red, Billie? Why, you've got red hair, so what are you grumbling at? It's not like you to pipe your eye for nothing. Come on now, tell Nurse Joyce.' And Mollie Joyce sat down on the edge of nine-year-old Billie's bed as if she had all morning to spare.

'Red hair, Billie – mine's red too; they used to call me "Firefly" at school. Did you have a nickname?'

'Yes, but I didn't like mine – ugh! "Carrots", they used to shout at me, and then I would chase them, so fast – as fast as a big racing hoop.' Then, after a pause . . . 'Donny has a red one.'

Nurse Joyce nodded. 'Yes, it's a beauty, he got it for Christmas. Lots of children have them – all the colours of the rainbow, so hurry and get strong then maybe you'll get one.'

She tried to sound convincing, but she felt the hopelessness of Billie's case too keenly, and hastily changed the subject.

'What did you get for Christmas?'

Billie continued to look glum. 'Just have a look in the locker by my bed,' he commanded.

It was a huge box of paints and a thick block of drawing paper. The parcel was still partly wrapped and the tag was still tied to it. 'With love from Mummy and Daddy,' it read.

Billie burst into tears. 'So you see, even Mummy and Daddy don't believe my legs will get any better. I'll never be able to walk again.'

Nurse Joyce was crying too as she gathered young Billie into her arms and rocked him gently.

'Just let's wait and see,' she murmured; 'just let's wait and see.'

At the back of her mind an idea was forming. Her nursing experience told her how important it is that the patient believes he can get better – if he has given up, he is less likely to improve. And Billie had obviously given up. She vowed to talk to the doctor and to Billie's parents at the first opportunity.

'Billie, I have an idea,' she said aloud. 'Why don't you paint me some pictures of the presents you'd really like to have got for Christmas. And be sure and use some nice bright colours. It's dinner time now, but as soon as you've finished that I'll get you some old papers and a big jar of water so you can start painting straight away.'

Billie cheered up a little at that. Nothing could stop him enjoying his dinner; and he really did want to please Nurse Joyce.

So, after dinner he opened up the paint box, took out the biggest brush and started to paint . . .

First he painted a bright red racing hoop.

Then a green one, and a yellow one . . . a blue one. He'd never seen so many colours as there were in that box of paints. Soon he had covered the page with dozens of hoops in a rainbow of colours.

Nurse Joyce saw what he was doing and came to admire them. 'But what else did you wish for Billie?' she asked.

'I'll show you,' said Billie; and he tore off the front sheet of paper. He rinsed out his brush and began to paint rapidly. There were bikes and scooters, hoops and skis. The he paused, brush poised above the paper.

'Skates,' he said. 'That's what I'd really like. Roller skates; so I could race along the pavement faster then anybody could possibly run.'

That night Nurse Joyce talked with the doctor. Her enthusiasm was infectious.

'If only we could get him some skates somehow, he might begin to believe he could get some use back in his legs,' she told them.

'Well, I don't know,' the doctor replied. 'But I could talk to the parents.'

'Oh, please do that; I really think it would help,' Nurse Joyce insisted.

The next evening at visiting time she watched covertly as Billie's Mum and Dad walked down the ward carrying a large parcel. It was wrapped in Christmas paper, though Christmas was long past. They wore secret smiles, betraying their hope for their son's recovery.

Billie stared. Why were his parents bringing a parcel today? Christmas had come and gone – it wasn't his birthday. Could it possibly be something to do with Nurse Joyce? Had she performed some magic overnight?

He didn't have long to wait.

His father hesitated when he reached Billie's bed, then handed him the package rather diffidently.

'We never thought you'd want skates, son, what with your legs being paralysed an' all. But if that's what you really want . . . here they are, shiny and new just like you told that nice nurse.'

'Oh, Daddy,' gasped Billie, 'I can hardly believe it. Can I try them on now?'

'Of course you can, lad.' His father's voice was a little gruff. 'Here, let me help you.'

And, while Billie quivered with excitement, his father pulled back the covers and fitted the new skates onto Billie's little feet.

'Now help me put my feet on the floor, Dad. Please, Dad?' he added, as his father hesitated again.

His legs felt very strange as they reached down and the skates touched the shiny linoleum; it had been such a long time.

'Hold my arm, Daddy.' he whispered.

His mother moved across to take his other arm, and together they supported him while he pulled himself up off the side of the bed and stood shakily between them. His knees were still a little bent as they moved slowly forward and the wheels turned beneath his feet.

Nurse Joyce watched, thrilled to see Billie out of bed at last. The other children gathered round.

'You know,' said Billie, 'I do believe I could learn to skate, if only somebody will help me practise every day, up and down the ward. And if I can learn to skate I guess I can learn to walk too.'

There was such a look of determination in his eyes that his Mum and Dad began to think maybe, just maybe, he could be right – no matter what the doctor said.

'Back to bed now, young Billie.' It was Nurse Joyce. 'You'll get all the help you need, I'll see to that, but right now you need some rest. Got to keep up your strength you know; it's going to be hard work. A little and often is the best way to practise.'

So Billie's Mum and Dad helped him back into bed, but he wouldn't let them take off his new skates. Instead, he lay with his feet poking out of the covers, where he could see reflections of the ward lights glinting in the shiny metal.

'I will learn to walk,' he promised himself, 'if it takes for ever'.

And with that he fell asleep.

# *Ermyntrude*

P.C. Woods presented himself at the headquarters, Moulstone, leading Ermyntrude. He looked rather sheepish.

'Brought her in on a charge of loitering, Sergeant: found her wandering about in the housing estate; apparently no fixed address'.

Sergeant Blum looked startled.

'Well, you go and find Bo-peep, and the sooner the better: we can't cope with Ermyntrude here.'

'Yes, sir,' said P.C. Wood smartly, and retired quickly, leaving his charge docile, but distinctly out of place in the Sergeant's office.

Sergeant Blum picked up the telephone and called, 'Any dogs in the pound to-day, Smith?'

'Yes sir, three, sir, all nice and quiet just now, sir.'

'Well come round and collect this woolly-bear, will you?'

Within two minutes Smith was eyeing the Sergeant and his companion somewhat doubtfully.

'What can I do with 'er sir?'

'Put her in the yard.'

'Can't do that, sir, the dogs would create bedlam. And what about 'er sir, she'd be frightened to death.'

'Oh, it won't be for long, Constable. Someone is sure to claim her pretty soon. But put her in the garden; anywhere but in here.'

So it came about that Ermyntrude took over the lawn in front of the police station.

She quite approved of the arrangement and children found it entertaining, but the pansies and the polyanthus were quite desolated.

Evening came and no anxious owner came to claim Ermyntrude, and the problem of where to accommodate her for the night became urgent. She could not be left on the lawn all night. There was a wood shed, of course, full of wood; there was the wash house too, but the Sergeant's wife objected to that; then there was the boiler-house: SHE would not like that, oh no!

'Oh, bring her in and put her in one of the cells for the night.'

Well, five days later, the lawn was finely cropped and Ermyntrude would have preferred to go back to the housing estate verges, but Sergeant Blum decided that she would have to be boarded out. So Mr. Wilson of Fawley Farm was invited to have her as a temporary member of his household. He had a large orchard where she would be able to meander in comparative freedom. He also had a black spaniel, a very friendly type, and fortunately she took quite a fancy to him and they were very happy there, for a short while; but then the spaniel got an urge to see more of the world, and he oozed through a gap in the hedge and his new companion followed where he led.

He nosed his way along the hedge bottom until they reached the main road, then, seeing a canine friend some distance away, he galloped off leaving poor Ermyntrude to wander indeterminately along the Queen's highway. She collected quite a mob of young admirers, and had to be taken in once again by P.C. Wood for causing an obstruction.

Now, when Sergeant Blum heard the front gate clang suddenly, he looked up from his desk and found himself face to face with Ermyntrude and P.C. Wood's blue helmet just disappearing round the hedge to the back.

He breathed noisily. The situation was ludicrous; it was getting out of hand, but he could not think of a solution.

He pushed up the bottom half of the window and leaned out on the sill, gazing with dislike at Ermyntrude, hoping for an inspiration; but she stared back – poker-faced; she didn't like him much either.

Dogs and cats! There were rules and regulations for dealing with them; one would know how to cope; but Ermyntrude – what kind of lost property would she be considered?

Shutting the window again, he tried to forget her temporarily and he went back to his books, and SHE went back to the herbaceous border.

In the next office P.C. Wood was engaged with a young person who was making some enquiries.

'Oh, it's six days since now. I had it in the shooting brake and it must have slipped out.'

And he wrote, 'Lost one fur coat, grey.' And then, looking up, 'Was it something like the one Madame is wearing now?'

At this she laughed 'Oh dear no, she's probably dirty and very bedraggled looking.'

'SHE,' cried Wood, almost bleating as the light dawned, and picking up the telephone he got through to Sergeant Blum.

'Sergeant, here's a lady to see you. Shall I bring her through? Urgent sir? Oh yes, indeed, sir; With pleasure, sir. Come through, will you Madame,' and with official dignity, rather spoiled by a large grin, he flung open Sergeant Blum's door and announced slyly,

'Bo-peep, Sir.'

# Grandar

'Why don't you come for a visit to us, Grandar, you could come by bus or train, either is convenient.'

The invitation had been given so many times in so many different ways, but always the answer had been the same: 'Nay, I'll not be going nowhere now I've lived all my life here, and what is left of it I won't be throwing away in one of them contraptions.'

And so the invitation had become mechanical and the reply just an echo of what Grandar had said on each of the previous occasions, and it was understood that Grandar would see no more of this world than he had seen as a boy, when he had sat behind the sturdy back of a cart horse on his way to the local market. His world was small, limited by his dislike and fear of 'them modern contraptions,' and perhaps, very soon, he would be called to the next world without having seen much of this one, for he was fast approaching eighty, and already living on the borrowed years.

His feet pained him at times, and felt too large for his laced boots, but he hobbled around the village and kept contact with his friends, and the outside world passed him by.

He winced visibly each time a motor horn sounded along the street and scowled at the man behind the wheel . . . muttering angrily, 'Deathtraps, that's what they are! I wouldn't like to be in one of *them* coming down Tonner's Hill; like as not their brakes would fail,' and after a moment 'but I hear London is a grand fine place.'

And he would look down at his feet as if there was still something of the Dick Whittington spirit left in him if not in his poor tired feet.

It was about this time that his grandson acquired a car, and the next time that the old man received the time-honoured invitation, he was there. Grandar gave the same old reply; but, just as everyone was settling down and expecting everything and everyone to go on as usual, the boy Nelson said, 'Would you come if we fetched you in the car, Grandar?'

Everyone sat up and took a new interest, there was a change, a new thread had been woven into the pattern.

'Nay, lad, nay. Naw I couldn't do that.' But there was change. He had looked startled, but excited; like a child seeing the unbelievable come within reach of his grasp just for a moment, and he had looked down at his feet on the hearth, he had looked out of the window as if he expected to see something parked by the kerb. But he shook his head.

'Naw, naw; well, not this time, mebbe some time, we'll see,' and he pressed his back into the old padded chair and stared hard into the fire.

Perhaps it was not just the firelight that put such a sparkle into those old eyes either. What had he said, 'London's a grand fine place'.

He didn't talk as much as usual that evening; and, after they had gone, he sat rather longer than usual, smoking what turned out to be an empty pipe. He went to bed, and bed didn't seem as comfortable as usual either. He tossed about a long time before he finally went to sleep.

During the next few weeks he seemed to take a sudden interest in local geography, in particular, Tonner's Hill.

How long was it since Jenner's lad had come clean over his handlebars into that field on one of those bad bends: my, it was a steep one that, and sharp corners too. He remembered well how the wagon had strained against the block brake as his horse eased it down the slope, stamping its hooves into the cobbly road to get a foothold.

Then that new fangled thing had come up from behind, pop-pop-pop . . . pop-pop-popping. He'd never seen anything like the way his old horse had dragged the wagon onto the top of that heap of broken stone. Both wheels had stuck on top, and its poor legs had been all of a tremble, poor thing. It was a wonder it hadn't fallen; and him too.

It was a few years since, mind you, ten or twenty, maybe forty years since he had been out that way.

He talked it over with Adam Rowley; he got about a bit, and Adam said, 'Oh ay, they've made a new road there now; it's that smooth, half the motors stick on the hill and the other half end up in the ditch at the bottom; I saw one meself . . . not long since neither.'

After that Grandar walked home with his chin on his chest, ruminating, not noticing the early daffodils that had already begun to fill the gardens.

He was thinking of Tonner's Hill.

It must be the worst bit of road in these parts; worst bit in England probably, well, he wouldn't be surprised. It must be a proper deathtrap. No, he'd never go in no car up that hill nor down it . . . it was a pity, though . . . because . . .

And with childish reaction he now felt defrauded of some long anticipated joy.

Funny, he wanted to go now, and they'd asked him for this year and he'd refused, and they only asked him once a year. Quite suddenly next year seemed a long way off. It was scarcely Spring yet, then all Summer and all next Winter before they asked him again.

He never noticed the postman standing outside his front door with a letter in his hand until a voice cried, 'A letter for you, George. I saw you coming up the street so I didn't drop it through the box. It's from them foreign parts; Henley – that's London, isn't it? That's where your eldest lives, isn't it. How is she now?'

The postman balanced one foot on the doorstep looking hopefully at the letter. But Grandar turned it over a few times, leaving the questions unanswered, and said, 'Thanks Tom,' and went inside.

He sat down in his chair for a few minutes looking enquiringly at his letter. They didn't write often. But eventually he took out his pipe and slid the stem under the flap and took out the letter.

It was from Nelson. No wonder he had not recognised the writing. He hadn't written before . . . ever.

Nelson was coming up north on business in his car; Nelson would call at Grandar's on Friday; Nelson would take Grandar back with him in the car – on Friday. Nelson said, 'Have your luggage ready.'

Luggage – he wouldn't need much. He'd get all he needed in a small bag. He'd take that old road map though that Adam Rowley had lent him. It might help the lad to find his way. He wouldn't know the roads so well in these parts. Then the spectre of Tonner's Hill raised its head and glared at him.

Excitement spent itself and he began to find excuses why he ought to stay at home; ridiculous at his time of life even to think of it. His rheumatism would be sure to catch him; his feet might let him down; but there, he wouldn't be walking, so he stifled that excuse. Friday was the day after tomorrow. Should he go, or shouldn't he? Painfully he wavered. Nevertheless, Friday found him with his small bag packed with a few necessities; his slippers taking up most of the space, and with a few bits and pieces in his pockets . . . and a paper bag of black and white mints, and two or three favourite pipes. It wasn't an ideal morning. There had been a frost overnight, and a slight mist hung among the branches and hid the sky, but, in spite of weather condition, Nelson arrived in good time, with Marion, his wife, in the front passenger seat, and Grandar was soon tucked in the back, and no-one was more surprised than himself.

The neighbours came to their front doors to wave. Old Adam leaned over his gate showing a rare interest. The children stopped their play and gathered round the car. They were giving him a grand send-off. He felt important, like royalty almost; he'd tell them all about London when he got back, if he ever got there, but there was Tonner's Hill to pass first.

And with that thought his body tensed, and he sat forward, silent, gripping the edge of the driver's seat with both hands as he realised he was inside one of those 'modern contraptions' – inside it, and it was carrying him away from all that he knew so well –towards Tonner' Hill and all its dangers, dangers which were magnified out of all proportion in his mind.

He watched for the landmarks as they came towards him out of the mist, the little church at the crossroads, the old mill with wide flung arms, a helpless giant today in the stagnant air; the group of trees . . . oh, they were not there . . . they must have been cut down. It was not more than a mile now: and then Grandar began to talk fast.

'It isn't far from here, Nelson lad; d'you think you can make it? You pass a farm on the right, and then the road turns suddenly to the left, and there's a ditch just round the bend; it's deep. You can't see it till you get round, then you turn right and the road goes up and up and up, you can't even see the top it bends round so, d'you think we ought to get out and walk . . ?'

Nelson felt some of Grandar's hysteria getting into his bones, his hands felt sticky and he wanted to mop his forehead . . . better to keep his hands on the wheel though.

Good gracious, he wasn't nervous; he'd negotiated hills that really were hills; Tonner's Hill was probably only an old man's mirage.

'Relax, Grandar, there's a good chap, we shall do it easily, no need to worry,' he said.

'It might be slippery; have you good brakes?' queried the old voice. 'You'll need to take care . . .'

'Goodness, this was awful, was the old man going to keep on and on; ice, yes, he must look out for that; bad bends too; steep hill, what if he crashed his gears; but he would't, why should he?'

'This is IT,' cried Grandar almost standing up in the confined back seat.

'There's the turn, there's the ditch, that's the field . . .'

Marion turned and gave him a push back into his seat for he looked as if he would seize the steering wheel at any moment and that would be disastrous.

Nelson took the first turn, nothing really difficult yet, round to the right, and up, yes that was a bad turn, but the little car was facing the hill bravely, bearing round to the right smoothly, and Nelson felt his confidence return as the gears slipped easily into third, and they mounted the last slope and topped Tonner's Hill without a hitch.

There was great sigh from the back seat as Grandar relaxed, and after a few minutes there was a rustling as his trembling fingers opened the paper bag of black and white mints and passed them to Marion.

Grandar's dragon had been thrown and he was on his way to London, Nelson was his St. George, and other dangers disturbed him not.

He smoked his pipe contentedly while the mist lowered and wrapped itself round the car and its occupants. Speed had dropped to a minimum and, while Nelson glared at the windscreen and his wife kept her eyes glued to the edge of the verge, Grandar knocked out his pipe into an old tin and put it away. Then, taking out a small box from one of his multitude of pockets, he produced a harmonica and was soon cheering them up with his music.

'Keep right on to the end of the road,' he played tunefully, for surely the lights of London were already visible through the fog . . . to Grandar at any rate.

# The Last Stitch

Primrose May was handmade, right to the last stitch. Miss Emily made her. She began with the stuffing and finished with the beautiful bonnet. From under the stiffened brim Primrose May's blue eyes looked out, across a little rainbow world of bits and pieces. She looked at Miss Emily's face, alight with pride and pleasure in her latest creation; Primrose May's pink silk floss lips smiled bewitchingly.

'There, that's the best yet,' said Miss Emily, and passed her across to Grandmama for inspection.

Grandmama inspected everything: she squeezed and pinched, and patted and pulled until Primrose May was quite out of breath.

'Woollen vest, silk knickers, embroidered petticoat, pink satin dress – and bonnet to match,' murmured Grandmama, checking off each garment; and everything takes off too.'

'Yes, indeed; everything – except the bonnet.' Before Grandmama had time to make loud, impertinent enquiries about the bonnet, a knock was heard on the downstairs door, and Miss Emily hurried away to answer it.

Grandmama's curiosity immediately swung back to the bonnet, and Primrose May wriggled quickly out of Grandmama's clutches. She slid down the steep, starchy apron front; bounced softly on the corner of the little wooden footstool, and rolled away across the rug as far as she could. She looked reproachfully at Grandmama from where she leaned against the table leg.

But she hadn't been quick enough. Grandmama was leaning well forward in her chair, her small, bony hands pressing the arms; her nose directed at Primrose May across the hearth, like an accusation.

Primrose May squirmed uncomfortably.

'Bald,' breathed Grandmama into the embarrassed silence. 'Bald as an egg.'

Poor Primrose May collapsed entirely and lay spread-eagled, half under the table and half across the edge of the rug.

Miss Emily, hurrying back into the room, picked her up and dusted her tenderly. 'There,' she sat her at the end of a row of dolls on the dresser, 'thank goodness she's no worse.'

As soon as Primrose May calmed down she saw the little Princess. She could just see her nose and a row of pink and white fingers on the edge of the dresser.

The little Princess had chosen *her*, immediately; she had scarcely looked at the others: and blue eyes looked into blue eyes lovingly.

'I must make her understand about the bonnet,' Primrose May thought to herself.

Then she began to feel uncomfortable again, and her rouged cheeks burned bright red. She looked across at Grandmama who was busy holding her rheumaticky old hands towards the blaze; and the firelight made the little Princess's curls shine like gold. *She* didn't wear a bonnet.

Presently Grandmama said, 'I can't get my hands warm; Emily get my hot water bottle, will you, please?'

Miss Emily obliged. She was used to Grandmama's sudden wants; and soon the old lady was patting her hands on a warm bottle, wrapped snugly in a yellow cover.

She began nodding. Miss Emily thought she was dropping off to sleep. But Primrose May knew she wasn't. Grandmama was up to something.

For a while Primrose May lay in the little Princess's arms, while a chubby finger threaded itself through the curls that lay primly across her forehead; or cork-screwed the little bunches of ringlets that fanned across her cheeks.

But she was much disturbed; and suddenly she flung her arms round the Princess's neck and peeped over her shoulder at Grandmama. Grandmama knew but Grandmama was still nodding.

She opened one eye, and winked, yes, she actually winked at Primrose May, and Primrose May opened her eyes so wide that her black cotton eye-lashes seemed extraordinarily long.

Why, Grandmama's eyes were twinkling – and suddenly Primrose May knew that everything was going to be all right.

Aunt Emily was looking for tissue paper. Tissue paper was a luxury in those days; why, even the bread was carried home naked. But then, Primrose May was to go home with a Princess, so several sheets were spread on part of the table, and Miss Emily wrapped her in the soft white folds, and Primrose May lay still – listening!

'Why Grandmama, you've unravelled your hot water bottle cover. It was quite new; and a beautiful colour.'

'I can't abide yellow,' grumbled Grandmama. 'I'll keep my old blue one,' and she wound the last bit of yellow crinkly wool on to a ball, and tossed it across to the table. It slipped in amongst the folds of white tissue paper, and Primrose May clutched it tightly all the way home.

Next day when the Princess took her to the birthday party, she took off her bonnet and everyone was delighted with her curls; curls all down the back, too.

How lovely of everyone –

How lovely of Grandmama, not to like yellow.

# A Night's Adventure

The little tin soldier had lost his musket. He had felt so proud this afternoon when Jeremy had complimented him on his smartness. They had been on parade, and he remembered how stiffly he had stood at attention. So stiffly, indeed, that he thought his knees would never bend again . . . and then they had all been hustled into the toy cupboard without even a 'stand-at-ease'. Usually, Jeremy took a salute and dismissed them quite properly, but somebody had said something about Cousin Christopher and the Zoo, and the army had been unceremoniously shoo-ed into the fort, and in the confusion he had lost his musket.

He had told the toys about it, and they were certainly sympathetic, but what could they do?

'I must creep out when all the grown-ups have gone to bed,' he said, but the golliwog shook his woolly black head.

'You won't be able to do that. You know the last thing Jeremy does is to come for ME, and he always closes the door after him,' said Golly.

And, of course, that was quite true. Little Tin Soldier felt perfectly miserable. What if they were called on parade tomorrow, as they very well might be, seeing as Cousin Christopher was here . . . and he without his musket? It was unthinkable.

Well . . . Jeremy must not be allowed to shut the cupboard door tonight, and that was that. It must be arranged somehow.

So the toys had a pow-wow.

Teddy said, 'Something must be jammed in the door just below the hinge.' He would be willing to hang his tail through the opening . . . but then, he hadn't a tail.

'What about Mouse?'

Mouse looked perturbed. Really, he couldn't run the risk of having his beautiful tail nipped off . . . and it might just happen . . .

'Oh, dear me, I simply couldn't,' murmured poor Mouse.

In the end they solved the puzzle by jamming the cricket stumps with their pointed ends through the gap between the door and the jamb.

Everybody cheered up then. Little Tin Soldier felt much happier, and settled down to wait until night.

It was later than usual when at last Jeremy came for Golly, and Christopher was with him.

'Would you like my teddy for tonight, I'll lend him to you if you like?' they heard him say, and then Christopher had said, 'No, thanks, but, I say, you've got some cricket stumps there, have you a bat? Oh, jolly good, we can play cricket tomorrow.'

Then Jeremy flung the door to, but it didn't shut . . ., not quite; so he pushed harder. But it wouldn't 'click' like it should.

'Look, it's the cricket stumps that are sticking out,' cried Christopher, and he pulled at the troublesome wicket and leaned it up against the wall of the fortress.

Little Tin Soldier was watching from the top of the wall, and he was almost in despair. The door would shut this time. He knew it would . . . then he wouldn't get a chance to get out . . . unless . . . Just as Jeremy flung the door to again, Little Tin Soldier leaned over and . . . he . . . pushed the cricket stump hard, and it fell down . . . down . . . down again. And it got wedged in the door once more.

'Oh, bother!' cried Christopher. 'We'll have to leave it till tomorrow,' and away they hurried to bed.

Very soon afterwards Little Tin Soldier slipped out of the fort, and crossed the little blue painted moat. The cupboard door was open. He climbed down the middle post and dropped softly onto the floor. Then he crossed the wide green carpet to the window bay . . . and there was his musket.

He was delighted. He swung it over his shoulder, and marched smartly round the window-bay all by himself . . . left – right . . . left – right.

Just then Jeremy's mother came into the room. Little Tin Soldier stood still; he hoped she would not see him. She didn't, but she noticed the open toy cupboard door, and Little Tin Soldier saw her remove the cricket stump and close the door quite firmly before going out of the room again.

So it seemed that his troubles were not over yet, even though he had his musket. He would be discovered 'out of bounds' next morning, and that would be a disgrace.

Slowly he re-crossed the wide green carpet until he stood quite close to the cupboard door. Looking up . . . up . . . up at the key hole. The key hole was halfway up the door; it was quite a big keyhole really, but it had never had a key in it as long as he could remember. He was sure he could squeeze through it . . . but, of course, he simply couldn't reach it. He stood looking at it a long time, then, suddenly he was so tired that he lay down just where he was . . . plop, and in spite of his sad predicament he fell asleep.

Now he hadn't been asleep very long when something wakened him.

Something was tickling his face. He rubbed it away, but in a few moments there it was, tickling his face again.

Oh, he was wide awake now . . . it was too dark to see what it was, so he just waited . . . and then it came again. It passed lightly as a cobweb over his face, and he stretched up his hand, s - l - o - w - l - y, and got it.

He held it for minute, then he laughed out loud — he was so glad — and he cried, 'How clever of them! How clever of the toys to think of this way to help me.'

There was Jeremy's whip cord dangling almost to his feet, safely threaded through the keyhole. Now, all he had to do was to climb up the cord and squeeze through the keyhole . . . and not even Jeremy would ever know about this night's adventure.

# Mr. Bumble

'Oh, oh, Mummy, Mummy, there's a bumble bee,' screamed Jenny, trying to scramble quickly to her feet and push the big furry creature away with her hands at the same time.

'My goodness, what a fuss you make!' growled an angry voice.

'Who said that?'

It had sounded quite near, but there wasn't anyone near. Mummy was in the middle of the field picking penny-moons, but it hadn't sounded a bit like her voice anyway. Jenny stayed very still, listening.

'Who is that talking? I'm sorry if I frightened you, but . . . where are you?' asked Jenny. 'I'm frightened too. I'm frightened of the bumble bee,' and she looked round to see where he was. She nearly screamed again when she saw him sitting on the strap of her sandal.

'*Don't* scream again . . . I can't bear it.' He buzzed excitedly. 'And don't stare as if you had never seen a bumble bee before.'

Jenny sat back and stared harder. Indeed, I have never seen a bumble bee that could talk before,' she explained. 'How extraordinary!'

'Well, of course, *I* am no *ordinary* bee,' he zoomed pompously. 'But please remember, even ordinary bees won't sting you if you don't frighten them. Now tell me, do you not admire my beautiful coat?' He got up and took a walk round her leg.

'OW!' cried Jenny sharply. 'I mean, oh, I think it is a most *elegant* coat, Mr. Bumble.'

'And do you not think the bright yellow bands around my middle are most distinguished?' he asked, taking another walk around her leg.

'They're . . . ha-ha-ha . . . lovely . . . ha-ha-ha,' giggled Jenny.

'Then, pray what are you laughing at' he demanded huffily.

'Oh dear, I'm so sorry, but you see you tickle my leg every time you walk round; and you do look rather silly wearing a thick fur coat on such a hot afternoon, Mr. Bumble.'

'I always wear my fur coat. I like it,' he answered buzzing furiously. 'It's time you went home, young lady.'

Jenny got up, carefully this time, but Mr. Bumble flew off to a tall nettle.

'Do mind the nettles, *they* sting!' she cried out.

'Nettles, oh, they won't hurt me,' he said, and he wriggled comfortable inside his thick fur coat. 'Besides, we are neighbours.'

'Do you mean you live next door to the nettles?' she asked, looking this way and that. 'I don't see your hive anywhere.'

'Hive, my dear, I have no hive. I am no *ordinary bee*. I have a nest and it is where clumsy cows and careless children cannot harm it,' and he disappeared underneath the nettlebed. Jenny could hear him buzzing down below.

'I expect Mrs. Bumble is there too, and perhaps a lot of little Bumbles. I wonder if they all wear their fur coats in the nest?' she laughed, and looked at the nettles . . . but they can't talk like bumble bees.

# *The Singing Tree*

Susan had found the singing tree the day before. She had been picking up some pretty bits of egg shell off the grass underneath the tree when she had heard the music; such tiny tinkling music.

She stood still listening. She was so still that the blackbird on the branch over her head didn't bother about her a bit. He was see-sawing gently up and down; his beak full of worms. Susan wished he would eat them up; they made his beautiful orange beak look untidy.

'Oh, that must be Mummy calling. It must be dinner time already,' and off she ran . . .

The blackbird squawked angrily and flew to the top of the tree.

He wished these humans wouldn't make him jump so. He'd lost quite half of his worms.

'Come along, Susan. Where have you been?' asked Mummy.

'I've been in the orchard listening to the singing tree,' she said.

'That sounds like a fairy tale. Trees don't sing, dear.'

'This one does, Mummy, right inside it,' she said, splashing away under the tap.

'Well, come and get your dinner now; oh, you had better put a clean pinafore on. I'll put this one to the wash,' said Mummy pulling the pinafore right over Susan's head.

'Can I have the pretty bits of shell out of the pocket, please? I think they are magic, Mummy. I found them under the singing tree.'

Mummy looked at them. She thought they were pretty too. They might even be magic.

'Mmmmm' she agreed, 'they are pretty; they look like Easter eggs for fairies.'

After they had cleared away the dinner things, and Susan had helped to polish the spoons, they went down to the orchard together . . . to see what they could see.

Susan skipped along, eager to show Mummy which was the singing tree. 'Look that's the one,' she cried, 'the one with the letterbox half way up the stalk.'

Mummy laughed merrily: 'You mean . . . Half way up the trunk . . . oh, oh dear.'

They *were* startled. A blackbird had suddenly streaked towards them under the low branches. He was screaming loudly. His beak was so wide open, and his tongue thrust out like a dart.

He looked terribly fierce.

'Oh bother,' grumbled Susan. 'We won't be able to hear the singing tree while he is making that noise.' There he perched in the very tree making such a fuss. He didn't seem to like *them* a bit.

They were disappointed, and were just turning away to go back to the garden when Susan cried excitedly, 'Goodness, Mummy, he has posted himself in the letterbox. I saw him.'

'Why, so he has . . . and look, here comes Mrs. Blackbird.'

She had her beak full of worms, and, when Mr. Blackbird popped out of the letterbox, she popped in.

Then the tree began to sing quite clearly, as Mrs. Blackbird fed her babies down in the secret hole in the very heart of the tree.

'Listen, Susan, five or six baby blackbirds singing for their supper . . . and it's *worms* for supper.'

# The Blue Ribbon Bow

It was only three days before Christmas when Santa Claus ran into trouble. The toys were all ready. There were hundreds of dolls; lady dolls, baby dolls, sleepy dolls and walkie-talkie dolls; there were hundreds of footballs and drums, cricket bats and trumpets, lorries, buses; and then the reindeer went down with flu.

They all had sneezes and temperatures, and Mama Claus put them to bed, gave them each a hot water bottle and tucked them in. She gave them hot lemon to drink with as much sugar in as they liked. They were very comfortable.

But Santa Claus sat on a stool, pulling his whiskers and thinking hard. He must find some other means of delivering the toys to the children. He thought and thought until it was long past his bedtime; and the clock struck twelve.

'Dong-dong-dong . . .'

Now just as the clock had 'donged' for the last time the fairy doll spoke. 'I will help you, Santa Claus,' she said. 'I will wave my magic wand over the toys so that they will all come alive. The horses will be able to gallop, and the dogs will be able to run. The dolls will be able to ride in the cars and the buses, and all the other toys can be piled on the trucks of the little engine.'

Santa Claus stopped pulling his whiskers and said happily, 'What a splendid idea.'

'There is one important thing, though,' added the fairy. 'All of us must change back into toys before the last stroke of twelve on Christmas Eve.'

So it was arranged, and very early on Christmas Eve a strange party set out with Santa Claus. He climbed into a toy helicopter so that he could see that everybody was getting along all right.

Mama Claus was at the door of Snow House to wave then off. Suddenly she hurried back inside and brought out a pretty blue ribbon which she tied round Teddy Bear's neck in a beautiful bow. Then they were off.

Everything went well. The toys slipped silently into the right stockings and settled down comfortably: all except Teddy Bear, and he turned stupid. He didn't like his beautiful blue bow. He wanted to wear a tie, and he said he wouldn't get into Jennifer's stocking.

He wouldn't even get out of the bus until it stopped at Peterjohn's house, and changed back into a toy. Then he climbed up beside Santa in the helicopter.

Teddy Bear was the very last of the toys, and Santa argued and argued with him, and even gave him some honey cough sweets to suck, out of a little red tin.

When they reached Jennifer's house they touched down on the pavement, and Santa Claus said, 'Be off now, Teddy, it's almost twelve o'clock. If you don't go now you'll miss Christmas. Why, listen!'

Just then the church clock began to strike – 'Dong!-Dong!-'

'Oh – bother!' cried Teddy, and tugged at the ribbon until it hung in two streamers down his front. Then he jumped quickly down on to the path, with the ribbons hanging down to his knees, scuttled up the drainpipe, and climbed on to the windowsill, but the ribbons would get in the way and all he could do was tumble right in, on to a nice thick rug. And that is where Jennifer found him the next morning.

'Now I expect SHE will make me a Beautiful Blue Bow,' he thought. But Jennifer didn't. She took the ribbon in her hands and folded it over and over and under and through . . . and made him a TIE.

And then Teddy was very very happy.

# *Christmas*

Mollie took hold of the knob with both hands, and turned it as softly as she could. It wasn't easy because her tiny hands slipped time and again on the shiny brass, and it was higher than her head, and she was cold. She had lifted the heavy chain off first, and left it dangling against the wall. She didn't bother about the huge iron key stuck in a draughty keyhole. No-one ever used the key here. Usually the hole was stuffed with rag or paper, but tonight the wind had blown out the stuffing and was finding its way through the thick scarf that Mollie had wound inexpertly round her neck.

Her head leaned over to one side as she strained and twisted, putting all her minute strength into the effort.

At last the door yielded; it rushed open, pushing her backwards as if it were angry with her for disturbing it so late at night . . . or perhaps it was early morning. Mollie didn't know.

She had heard Tailly barking. Poor Tailly, all alone down in the cowshed . . . all alone except for Daisy and Dandy. She had wanted to rush straight out and get him and bring him in, but it had been snowing so hard she could not see through the window. She had stood there, listening to his high pitched bark that seemed to fill in the gaps between the wind's excited chorus. But she had crept back to bed, cold and very wide awake.

Then the snow had stopped. The sky had cleared . . . the feathers that had whirled and capered in the tempestuous wind had disappeared. Now a star twinkled at her through her window . . . and, then she was pulling on her coat, boots, a scarf, and struggling with the heavy old farmhouse door.

She tightened the scarf, and held her coat, unbuttoned, across her middle with one hand, pulling the door closed after her with the other.

Seconds later she was half running, slipping and slithering along the rough path that led up the slope to the cowshed. It wasn't far from the house but it was almost hidden by the hill, and the familiar ruts and stones in the path were camouflaged by the moonlit beauty of newly fallen snow. Its roof was sheeted with snow, sparkling in the uncanny light. All around was sheeted with snow; everywhere sparkled; everywhere was light.

So, she didn't notice the light glowing in the window, she only knew that, now, Tailly was quiet.

He must have curled up in the little hay bed that she had made for him and gone to sleep after all. Perhaps he had been afraid in the darkness . . . But it was light now. She wasn't frightened either. Her boots were making deep holes in the snow. Each one seemed deeper than the last. Already she sank knee deep, and it was deeper still near the door where the wind had driven the snow a short while ago.

Her legs were wet. The bottom of her coat was wet. Oh, tomorrow it would be Christmas.

She'd get Tailly and hurry back.

She plunged into the last mound, and grasped the handle of the small inlet door, and as she pressed the lever it opened with a sharp click. She stood still, alert and expectant. Tailly's sharp ears would be sure to catch even that small sound. He would yelp in welcome . . . he would come hurtling across the stone floor and fling his fat little brown body into her arms. But nothing happened . . . all was quiet except for the low mooing of Daisy and Dandy as they murmured in their sleep.

It was then that she noticed the light.

It was coming from the third stall, past Daisy, past Dandy; it was coming from the disused stall, the one where she had piled the straw, bolstering it round with pieces of wood, and making a cosy nest for Tailly, her new puppy. Stepping over the wooden ledge into the shed she tiptoed towards the strange light. Daisy swished her tail gently as she passed; Dandy tramped softly on her bedding with dull thuds. They were awake, content and patient, and Mollie crept on till the third stall lay in full view. A storm lamp hung from a hook illuminating a strange scene.

Tailly was there, snuggled up beside a tiny child, and the child lay asleep in the little hay bed.

She made her way back to the house in a daze. She didn't know that she was smiling, that her face was lit up with wonder.

They met her on the doorstep . . . and they weren't angry.

Mollie said, 'It's Christmas, isn't it?'

And Mummy said, 'Yes, dear, yes, of course. Yes, it's Christmas,' and she drew Mollie into the warmth, with gentle concern.

'There's a baby in the cowshed,' whispered Mollie, and shivered ecstatically.

They put rugs round her, gave her hot drinks, and after a while she fell asleep, with the smile still on her lips.

Suddenly a knock on the door startled them. A man, apologising for the intrusion, asked for milk . . . 'For the baby,' he said. They'd used all they had brought with them. Their car was stuck in a drift just down the road. They'd taken the liberty of entering the shed. Nice and cosy they were. Nice little terrier pup in there too.

'Hope we shall be able to dig the car out in the morning and get on the way again.' He turned to go, and then, waving his hand inclusively round the snowy scene, cried, 'Thanks for the milk. Merry Christmas.'

# The Christmas Card

Janie untied the string which had held them together, and began placing the cards amongst the photo frames and bits of bric-a-brac that had collected through the years.

They were old now, her cards, and old-fashioned just as she was. She didn't expect any new ones – there hadn't been any for years. Nobody remembered her now: there was nobody left to care.

Whimsically, she fitted two of the cards into old envelopes, pushed the flaps inside, and dropped them on the mat under the letter-box. She pretended not to notice they were there as she went through into the bedroom . . .

The moment she woke up she knew it was Christmas morning, and she lay still for a while, eyes closed, remembering. Folk said you couldn't remember your childhood, but Janie could. Sometimes it seemed more real than the present.

When she was a child she had always thought that the most wonderful moment on Christmas morning was when the envelopes poured through the letterbox like a deluge, splashing down on to the mat. But the deluge had become a trickle, and now she might just as well not have a letterbox, there was never anything but the gas bill. Sometimes when the wind was strong the flap would rattle teasingly and she would stop whatever she was doing and listen . . . wondering if there might possibly be a letter from somebody . . . anybody . . . dropping on to the mat.

Moving as quickly as she could, because it was cold, she slid out of bed and into her clothes, putting her old dressing-gown on top of everything to keep her warm until she got the fire going.

It had snowed during the night; she saw the thin layer of glittering white when she pulled back the curtains, and she shivered as she went through into the living room and picked up the two white oblongs that were still just where she had dropped them on the mat. Last night it had seemed a joke to put them there, but in the chill light of morning, somehow, the joke misfired. She didn't even go through the pretence of opening them. She put them on the table and went across to the hearth to light the small gas fire, and then the gas ring with the same thrifty match.

Janie began making her porridge. She would feel better once she was warm. She stared hard into the pan, stirring steadily, careful not to look towards the window where the snowy brightness reminded her that it was Christmas. What an old silly she was, she thought, as a tear dripped into the pan.

Suddenly there was flip and then . . . flop. And a small white square was lying on the mat.

She stared at it incredulously. Then, carefully balancing the pan on the ring, she went towards it, stealthily, almost as if at any moment it might disappear.

It *was* a Christmas card . . . and it *was* for her. It said, Miss Janie, on the front, in sprawly red crayon letters, and inside a card challenged her 'Merry Christmas', and a spray of holly glowing with bright red berries filled the rest of the space.

'Lovely! Why, it's beautiful. Who can have sent it?' Janie was puzzled. On the back it said quite distinctly, 'With love from Timmy.' But who was Timmy?

She carried it across to the table, leaned it against the sugar basin, and took another look at the envelope. It was very small, and the stamp wasn't a real one . . . red crayon again. She smiled as she thought of her own little postman. What was he like?

She ate her breakfast and enjoyed it.

In the distance church bells were ringing.

There was voice calling outside, young and shrill.

'Timmy! Timmy!'

Janie hurried to the door in time to see a red woolly cap like a tea cosy bob up from behind a fence, and a small boy, his cheeks glowing with the cold air, his red gloved hands full of snow, set off running towards home.

'Merry Christmas!' he shouted as he passed her, and Janie cried, 'Merry Christmas, Timmy!'

She remembered now . . . she had seen the furniture van only a few days ago. Timmy and his family must be her new neighbours – yes, there he was, turning in at the gate next door, and her front path was dappled with small footprints.

Janie went indoors. She was warm now, warm deep inside. Christmas had come again, with snow, and holly, and church bells, and love . . . from Timmy.

# Norman

## Nothing but the Truth

As a small boy the need to tell the truth was instilled into me very thoroughly. To tell lies was likened unto stealing. My grandfather, a local preacher with a long white beard, would proclaim, 'Tell the truth and shame the devil!' I was duly impressed and in my small way I tried to live up to his teachings. This did not make me very popular when I refused to say I liked rice pudding, or Sunday School or even Aunt Polly, but I consoled myself with the thought that the way to heaven is not an easy one – at least so Grandad said.

Then I went to school and again the theme was, 'Honesty is the best policy!' 'Tell the truth, own up to your misdemeanors, and your punishment will be light!' Again I did my best. And if some of my pals got away with all kinds of things and laughed when I owned up and was punished, I was fortified inside, and when the soreness of my beatings wore off I felt quite a hero.

This was all right, but I was beginning to get a reputation among my family and acquaintances for being eccentric, and as I grew up I made more enemies than friends. The truth so often hurts, and, although I realised this, my early teaching would not allow me to stretch a point. If I was asked how I liked somebody's painting or model, or even girl friend, I did not hesitate to say it was lurid, or crude or unpleasant when that was my opinion.

Then came the time when I had to start work. Fortunately, my school report was good. After all, I had taken my lessons seriously, and my headmaster could not but say that I was 'truthful and straightforward' even if I was not particularly bright. With this report I soon got a job with a firm of accountants, and I thought I was on the threshold of a fine career.

Alas, within a week I had given mortal offence to the boss's private secretary by refusing to admire her new hat, which was, in fact, like a lampshade; I had told a client that the boss was playing golf, and I had frankly confessed to an arithmetical error which I could have easily rectified without anybody being any wiser.

It could not last. When my trial period came to an end I was told to take my 'truthful and straightforward' character elsewhere.

This time it was not so easy. Prospective employers are so inquisitive. 'Why had I left the accountants – such a good prospect?' Of course, I told the truth. Whether I was believed and considered unsuitable or merely regarded as an unmitigated liar I don't know. The effect was the same – no job for me.

Ultimately a local greengrocer who knew my father was persuaded to give me a chance. I worked hard behind the scenes from Monday till Friday moving boxes of fruit and vegetables around, sorting, cleaning up and generally making myself happy to be busy, but on the Saturday I had to help with sales in the shop. I didn't mind this, but what could *I* say when customers asked, 'Are the grapes sweet?' 'Are the lettuces fresh?' 'Are the tomatoes sound?' Naturally I told the truth – plain and unvarnished! Equally naturally I was soon out of a job again, and the prospects were very glum.

All this time I was developing an antagonistic frame of mind. The world didn't like me because I spoke the truth, and I didn't like the world because I heard so many lies. At least I regarded them as lies, and I began to pick on slight inaccuracies of word and fact which people said, and made a major issue of each one of them. Moreover, I was not always right! One day, after one such incident, when I had been involved in a fight with an old friend after calling him a liar because he said a certain train left at five past one when I was sure it left at five to one, my father asked me to go for a walk with him.

My father was a solicitor, and a very busy man, and did not give a lot of his time to his children, so I was rather surprised at this request, but I made no demur and soon we were tramping along the country road which leads from our house to the river.

Very little was said until we got to the river bank, where we sat on the grass and watched the water, then my father started. 'John,' he said, 'I think it is time that you and I had a chat. I have been worried about you lately. You know how busy I am and how little time we have together. But I am your father, and, moreover, I am very fond of you and would like above all things to see you happy. Come, tell me your troubles – you never know – I may be able to help you.'

When my father talked like this, it was obvious why he had become not only the senior partner of a famous firm of solicitors but also the confidant and friend of some hundreds of clients.

Haltingly at first, and then more fluently as Dad prompted me, I poured out my tale of woe – my story of the wickedness of the world and the goodness of me.

When I reached the end, Dad did not laugh, as he might well have done. Instead, he took my arm and said, 'Let's walk along the river bank. I can think better that way.'

After a while he stopped. 'Grandad is at the bottom of this,' he said. 'He was a grand old man but he was too fond of catch phrases – "Tell the truth and shame the devil". 'He would be the first to tell you that you must first find the truth, and that you cannot do without knowing both sides of a question. It is a feature of English law that a man must be regarded as innocent until he is proved guilty. You have condemned people without trial. You have thought that there could be no excuse for a lie. Let me tell you, my boy, the world would be a very weary place if everybody spoke the truth, the whole truth and nothing but the truth the whole time.

'If Grandma had asked Grandad whether he liked her new hat, do you think he would have said ''No!'' Not likely; not even if it did look like a lampshade. He knew, as I know, and as I want you to know, there is sometimes a case for mild compromise – occasions when truth can be tempered with tact. I am not suggesting that you should agree with people indiscriminately, or hesitate to stand up for what you know is true and good, but the examples you have given me could have been dealt with tactfully without any harm to anybody – and perhaps a little good. We should not hurt others for the sake of principles which may be only pride.'

My father's words sank deep. He had not told me off, he had spoken to me as one man to another and I was impressed.

We walked home in silence, each with our thoughts, and as we got near the house I heard my young sister practising on the piano. When we opened the door she rushed to me and said, 'Come along, John, and listen to my new piece!' I allowed myself to be led into the sitting room and sat down while she struggled haltingly through *Minuet in G.* Then she asked me somewhat doubtfully, 'Wasn't that nice?' My immediate reaction was to tell her the truth, then I caught father's eye on me. 'Er – er, you're improving, Peggy!' Her eyes lit up. 'Oh, I *am* glad *you* think so, John,' and she gave me a spontaneous kiss.

This was my first attempt to temper the truth with tact and the reward was sweet. I could not sleep that night as I wondered, 'Was I courting the devil instead of shaming him?' After all, what I had said was Nothing but the Truth.

# The Calendar

Are you interested in calendars?

Not much – well, neither am I.

Lots of them used to arrive in December each year at the office where I worked. They were sent by firms with whom we did business – large ones, small ones, beautiful ones, some quite artistic, others just straight-forward advertisements. My choice, invariably, was the type with a leaf to tear off each day of the year, preferably with mottoes or short sayings printed below the date.

I made a habit every day when I arrived at the office of tearing off yesterday's leaf and reading the few words for today. I had a rigid rule never to look forward to what was coming in the future. It is surprising how these little sayings can colour your life.

This happened to me.

One morning I arrived at the office early, as usual, but feeling very down. I had not slept well, my head was aching and I had indigestion. My staff were in for a rough time. Wearily I tore off yesterday's page from the calendar and read the quotation for today:

    'Let me be a little kinder,

      Let me be a little blinder

        To the faults of those around me.'

This made me think.

At that time I was the Deputy Head of a large department and I was never 'blind to the faults of those around me'. I was ambitious and aimed to be the

Head as soon as the old man retired. I worked hard myself and made everybody else do likewise. I checked everything carefully, no stop or comma must be omitted from my letters, all figures must be correct to the last decimal place. There must be no alterations. Any errors had to be re-typed even though the culprit had to work late. Punctuality was essential and any late-comers or early-leavers got a good telling-off and warning.

I was not popular but the boss appreciated my value and had hinted that he would recommend me for promotion in due course.

When I read the calendar, I wondered. Was I getting the best out of life? I took work home most evenings, I was tired and could not sleep, I suffered from headaches and indigestion. Was it worth it?

The old man was not really old but he was retiring on account of ill health. Would I be wiser to be a 'little kinder, a little blinder', even if I remained a Deputy for the rest of my life?

My reverie was interrupted by a gentle knock on the door.

'May I come in, sir?' It was Jones – 'Charlie' to his friends. He was a cost clerk and was always very quiet and subservient when he came to see me although sometimes I heard him laughing and joking with his friends.

'I'm sorry I'm late, sir, but my wife is ill and I had to get the children off to the school.' I started to tell him that if he wanted to keep a nursery he needn't bother to come to work, then I pulled myself up. 'A little kinder!' Instead, I said, 'Oh, yes, Jones, I'm sorry to hear that – er – how are you going to manage at tea time? Do you want to get away early?' Was this me talking?

Obviously, Jones was a bit overwhelmed as he replied, 'Oh yes, SIR, that would be a great help.'

I settled down to work feeling quite self-righteous and throughout the day tried to be tolerant to everybody although the habits of recent years were hard to break and my patience was tried many times. I was pleased, however, when several of the staff smiled at me when they said 'Good night' at the end of the day.

When I arrived home, carrying a brief case of homework, as usual, my wife said that she wanted to have our meal quickly, as she intended to visit her mother who was ill. I started to grumble, then remembered 'a little kinder'. I enjoyed that meal – my wife was always a good cook but I said, 'Would you like me to go with you to see your mother? We could take her some of my chrysanthemums out of the greenhouse.' 'Oh, yes,' said my loved one. 'Mother would love to see you and she does like your flowers, but what about all that work in your briefcase?'

'That can wait till tomorrow,' I said, and her loving kiss was my reward.

I never became the boss but I made many friends and enjoyed my life as a Deputy. Was this because I took so much notice of the calendar?

> 'Let me be a little kinder,
> Let me be a little blinder
> To the faults of those around me.'

# The Impromptu Speech

It was the Music and Arts Festival of the Beverley Methodist Circuit and, wishing to support Norwood Church, I had entered for the 'Impromptu Speech'.

When I arrived at Toll Gavel I was ushered into a side room and there I met the other competitors. There were thirteen of us, nine men, three ladies and me.

We were asked to take a folded piece of paper from a box and told that the numbers thereon would determine the order in which we were to speak.

I drew number thirteen and realised I would have a long wait.

I tried to make conversation with my fellow competitors but they were not very interested in trivialities – mostly they were very tense as though awaiting an ordeal. I tried to interest myself in the various handwork samples which were spread on the tables in the room but this soon palled and I was relieved when number one was called to make his speech in the big hall next door. It seemed a long time before we heard some clapping and there was another interval before number two was called.

I calculated that it would be nearly an hour before I was called and I began to wonder why I was there at all. As I pondered, memories came back of factors which had given me the ambition to become a great orator. I recalled a preacher, John Cox, at the Union Street Methodist Church in Middlesbrough where my grandfather used to take me as a boy. The Rev. Cox was a white-haired rosy-faced man of ample proportions and, as he enthused over the glories of heaven or the terrors of the other place, he would wave his arms about and become redder and redder till I wondered whether he would burst. I smiled as I thought of him, and then number three was called.

I began to realise that thinking about the past would be a good way of passing the time and went back into my reverie.

The next speaker to come to my mind was the Reverend Dr. Bradley in Darlington. He was a very different type, rather aristocratic but lucid, and when he recited Gunga Din at parties he made the story come alive and his sermons were not soporific. As I remembered him, number five was called. Good, I must have missed number four.

I tried to recall my next mentor. The headmaster at my school. He was plump and his bald head came nearly to a point at the top. The boys nicknamed him 'The Egg' and it fitted his portly shape admirably but he also could talk eloquently.

On Sunday evenings a service was held in the school and usually The Egg preached a sermon. Often he read a sermon written by some celebrity but sometimes he used his own words and this was much more interesting as he was able to encourage those who were doing well and urge the sluggards to greater efforts. I thought 'he would be worth emulating'.

When I was a little older I took part in school debates but was invariably outshone by some bright spark with a quicker mind than mine. I was thrilled, however, on one occasion to be asked to propose a vote of thanks to a guest speaker and regarded the round of applause which followed my speech as being at least in part for me.

As I matured I became a regular participant in discussions at professional meetings and even presented a paper on a subject with which I was very familiar.

My thoughts jumped as the sound of clapping brought me back to earth and soon there was a call for number seven. Good – or was it good? None of my speaking in public could be regarded as 'impromptu'. Was I going to make a hash of it?

No, surely. I remembered the witty speech I had made when opening the Spring Fair and how well my efforts at the Sunday School anniversary had been received.

Nevertheless, I became more and more nervous as my companions left me one by one until I waited alone for my call.

At last my turn came and I entered the large Sunday schoolroom where I was greeted at the door by a man who gave me a piece of paper on which was written three subjects. I was told that I must choose one of these for my speech. I looked at the paper, handed it back and walked across the platform. Then I looked towards the audience. There seemed to be a lot of people and my eyes began to mist over. What could I say to entertain them? I tried to remember what it said on the paper but it had all gone from my mind. I dashed back to the man at the door and there was a titter from the audience. I took the paper and placed it on the lectern and a voice said, 'You must start now and you will have two minutes.' I started, 'Ladies and Gentlemen,' and there I stopped. I had no idea what to say about any of the subjects on the paper. The silence as I tried to gather my thoughts was frightening, and then it came to me. I would tell a funny story. Perhaps it would have some relevance to one of the subjects. So I broke the silence and started into my story. It was a good story and I thought I was telling it very well but just as I was getting to the crucial point a bell was rung and I was told that my two minutes was up.

I sat down and awaited the verdict of the adjudicator. This was short, sharp and to the point. 'This speech was quite irrelevant and no marks will be awarded.' I was downcast. Then a voice came from the audience, 'Can we hear the end of the story?'

The adjudicator agreed to this and I mounted the platform again. This time I had lost my nerves and gave the rest of the story in good style. Everybody laughed at the conclusion and the audience cheered as I returned to my seat determined never to try to make an impromptu speech again.

# The Light at the end of the Tunnel

I was very pleased when the chief surveyor told me to go down the pit and take the air measurements by myself. It was not a very difficult job but it meant taking responsibility. I had to go to a number of places in the pit and measure the air flow with an anemometer.

It proved a bigger job than I had expected, not taking the readings, although this was awkward enough, holding my lamp and the anemometer and looking at my watch, but the places were a long way apart and by the time I was nearing the end it was getting late. I decided to take a short cut. It was only about a mile along the air road from my last point to the pit bottom and it was three miles by the travelling road. I knew there must be a way through: the wind came along strongly and air roads are inspected regularly by the pit deputies. I couldn't get lost – all I had to do was to keep walking with my face into the wind.

I hadn't got very far when the going became difficult. The roof came down so that I had to walk in a sort of crouched position, but worse was to come. There was a fall or rock across the road; I shone my light into the cavern and I could see broken pit props. Bits of stone were falling intermittently but there seemed to be a way over the top. Taking my courage in both hands I decided to try to get over. There was just room and I slid down the other side on my back. I was congratulating myself – and then it happened. I dropped my lamp and it went out. I groped around and found the lamp but it wouldn't light. I twisted the switch this way and that, tried banging it, but all to no avail. No doubt the bulb had broken. It was dark, such darkness as I had never imagined. I closed my eyes and opened them: there was no difference.

What was I to do? If I stayed there it might be days before anybody found me. It was Friday and I might not be missed till Monday. I had nothing to eat or drink with me and, besides, I was right on the edge of a fall of stone – more might come any time. This blackness was terrible. I began shouting for help, then reason prevailed. I began to talk to myself. 'Norman, my boy, this is where you are up against it but it is no use panicking.' 'All right,' I said to myself, 'but what can I do?' 'Have faith, my boy. You know that if you keep going into the wind, you must land at the pit bottom.'

I slung the anemometer round my neck, hung the useless lamp on my belt and, stretching both hands in front of me, crouched well down and lurched towards the wind. I got about ten yards, then something hit me above the eyes. I went down like a ninepin. I rubbed my forehead – it was wet but I could not tell whether it was blood or sweat. I put my hand up to feel what had hit me. It must have been a girder. Lesson number one: keep your head lower than your hands.

On again – every now and again I had to bend almost double to get along but I was finding the height of the roof with my hands and, even though I had to crawl at times, I was making progress. After what seemed an age of struggling at last I saw in the distance a glimmer of light. It must be the pit bottom. I stood straight up in delight – crack went my head against the roof and down I came again. The lesson learnt, I went forward carefully but it was easy now. The light ahead was like a star which grew bigger and bigger as I got nearer.

Many times in later years I have remembered this experience and it has helped when things seemed very black to realise that with faith there would be a light at the end of the tunnel.

# The Water Diviner

Suddenly he became conscious that his arms ached, and he lowered the paper to his knees. He folded it, but kept his thumbs between the sheets as he stared into the little fire in the grate.

'Yes,' he murmured to himself, 'I can do it. £1,000 for marking the spot. Why, Ellie could have the lessons then, bless her. How her mother would have loved to see her now. The child seemed to draw magic out of the old piano. She should have her chance. He would be able to buy her a new one . . . She should have the best teachers . . . Yes, he would do it.

Old Simon got up from his favourite chair in the corner by the fireside, and began to take cups down from their hooks. She would be in any minute now; he'd get the cocoa ready and they would be off to bed early.

He was tired and he stoked an invisible lock of hair back from his high forehead, thinking of his early morning efforts.

The common had seemed a long way to his old legs, much further than he remembered.

He had been up with the grey of dawn with his pencilled plans . . . a thick blue scarf wound round his neck. Ellie had knitted it for him.

'To match your eyes,' she had said affectionately.

In the early hours he had taken the sensitive hazel twig and walked the area marked on his plan, and in his fingers it became a live thing revealing to him the secrets of the water that lay hidden hundreds of feet below. And he was satisfied that he could solve the Mayor's problem.

Seven o'clock the following evening found him standing just inside the council chamber of Bonniton Town Hall. The heavy doors had swung silently to behind him. His entry had passed unnoticed.

'Gentlemen, the situation is intolerable,' the Mayor was saying wearily. 'Southcombe are more than willing to provide us with water . . . at their price. But their price is exorbitant. Our townsfolk would be up in arms; still they threaten to disrobe us if we cannot find some means of providing them with water they so desperately need. £1,000 I have offered . . . £1,000. Gentlemen, think . . . think . . .'

But the anxious faces of the councillors showed no hint of inspiration. They had racked their brains until they ached.

Then, into that gloomy atmosphere stepped Old Simon, map in hand. To their astonishment he laid his map on the table and pointed to a blue cross with the simple words: 'Bore, there. I tell you, you will find water in plenty at a depth of 200 feet. When you have your water, I will return for my fee.'

And then he was gone.

They stared incredulously at the place where he had stood; it was as if they had seen a ghost . . . but the map lay where he had put it, on the polished surface of the great table, and the blue cross indicated a place they all knew well.

So great was their relief that they forgot to question the stranger's knowledge, his uncanny appearance . . . they even forgot to ask his name. And as for the £1,000, well, that could wait.

It was not long before 'Blue Cross' was teaming with activity. Men with tapes . . . men with shovels . . . men with lorries; the necessary framework was erected and the boring began. The once green and gold turf was churned up, and ugly heaps of earth sprang up all around; but the work progressed with all speed. Then one day they reached mud, brown sticky sludge that meant the precious water was within their grasp.

Gladly they carried on, until, at last, the coveted water was flowing through newly-laid pipes to the homes of Bonniton people; water gushed from their taps, sparkling and plentiful.

The Mayor and his councillors once again gathered in the council chamber; this time to congratulate themselves on a job well done. They took their seats, smiling at one another affably. The Mayor leaned across his desk, his chain flapping gently on the thick minute book, as he began: 'Gentlemen . . .'

The atmosphere was warm. Outside the sun was shining. They had had no rain for a week, but water was no problem now.

Almost noiselessly then the heavy swing doors opened, and Old Simon was standing just inside. In his hand he held his hat, revealing an intelligent face lit by a pair of keen blue eyes.

He wasted no words. 'The contract is accomplished,' he said briskly. 'You have your water supply. Now, if you please, my fee of £1,000.'

Shocked, the Mayor cried, 'A £1,000, for a blue cross on a map! Indeed, we have done the work . . . we have paid already. Come, take £50, my man. It is a most generous offer.'

Old Simon's eyes hardened. So . . . they would not pay . . . they did not intend to keep their promise. Very well, then, he knew what he knew, and in a steely voice that his Ellie would not have known, he said, 'Today you will not pay, but take heed lest tomorrow you pay another way.'

It might have been a draught from the swinging doors that caused those worthy citizens to shiver; certainly the scorned cheque lifted lightly, and fluttered across the polished table, where it lay accusingly, face upwards in front of the Mayor.

No one noticed Old Simon leave the building. With his bowler hat well down on his ears and his chin on his chest he was an insignificant little figure.

Too late the councillors realised how little they knew of him. Fear gripped them . . . a stupid, superstitious fear; it was ridiculous. But it was too late then . . . 'Too late for what?' they questioned.

They didn't know; but when Blue Cross Hole ran dry, they felt it was HIS doing: and, as they paid Southcombe's price for water, they felt that HE was at the bottom of it.

And who's to say that it was not so?

For, later, it transpired that Southcombe had a new bore hole, all of 300 feet deep, and not more than a mile or so beyond Bonniton Common, where the Blue Cross scarred the landscape . . . a useless memento of a broken pledge.

And Ellie got her piano, and became a great pianist . . . so, who knows?

# The Toast of the Guests

'What about Billy?'

I pricked up my ears; it was the football club committee meeting and we were discussing arrangements for the annual dinner dance. I say 'we' advisedly for, although I never took an audible part in the discussions, I was there. I was not a good player but I had always been there – ready to fill a vacancy in the reserves or act as linesman or to help the others with their kit. The main thing was, I was one of the club and when I became a member of the committee my cup was full and running over.

Now they were short of somebody to propose the toast to the guests at the dinner. None of the other members of the committee were willing, and the chairman was really pulling my leg when he said, 'What about Billy?'

There was a quick laugh round the table, but it wasn't unfriendly to me, and my pal Sam Jones said, 'Why not? I'll bet Billy would make a jolly good job of it.' Nobody wanted to argue and prolong the meeting, so it was agreed.

When I arrived home, I shouted to my wife, 'Sally, I'm going to make a speech at the club dinner.'

Sally came into the room: 'They must be short of somebody to ask. You've never made a speech in your life.'

'Well, p'r'ps not,' I replied, 'but I have often wanted to and this is my chance.'

'Please yourself,' said Sally, 'but don't make a fool of yourself and me in front of all those people.'

As I ate my supper I had a little glow of anticipation inside me. I'd show them – and Sally too.

The next day I called at the library; there was a good selection of books written for the express purpose of transforming the tongue-tied into orators and I picked out two. Sally teased me when she saw the books under my arm but she was going round to her mother's and left me in peace.

I studied the books and then got busy with pencil and paper. Words came easily – a sincere welcome to our guests who would be mainly benefactors of the club – thanks for their past good work and anticipation of future help – a topical reference to a recent victory – hopes for the next cup-tie – a mention of Wembley that would bring a laugh. I scribbled on happily; time passed quickly and I was still busy when Sally came home and chased me off to bed.

Every day that week I used so much paper, writing, altering and re-writing that Sally said she would start a bonfire. Eventually I finalised my ideas, checked the timing and set about memorising the speech.

I went for long walks on the beach and recited out loud to the waves. I had read that famous orators used this method to practise their voices. Not that my voice was weak – my shouts of 'Come on the REDS – FOUL or OFFSIDE' could be heard from one side of the football ground to the other.

When the evening of the dinner arrived, I was word perfect and quietly confident; but I had written my speech on small cards and put these in my dinner jacket pocket, just in case.

Sally and I had been allocated places at the top table, not in the centre, of course; in fact, we were at the far end, but I was content.

I looked at the menu but was more interested in the toast list than what we were going to eat, and, sure enough, there I was in print. I wanted to turn to everyone and say, 'Look – that's ME.' Even Sally was a bit impressed.

I turned to one of my neighbours, the guest who was to reply to my toast and said, 'Awful bore, having to make a speech.'

'Oh, I don't know,' he replied. 'I don't mind making speeches. It is listening to them which bores me.'

The Chairman rose to propose the Loyal Toast, then called upon the Mayor to propose the toast of the football club. He had no notes and, apparently nothing to say but certainly he said it. Memories of the club's victories, defeats, problems, anecdotes. I looked at my watch – 15 minutes, 20, 25, 30. Would the man never sit down? At last the end came and the toast was drunk.

The Chairman had also been watching the clock and very soon he asked the Vice-chairman to reply on behalf of the club. My heart began to flutter; there were butterflies in my tummy. It would soon be my turn.

The Vice-chairman started well. I wondered whether he and I had studied the same books. Then he decided he ought to reply in detail to the Mayor's remarks. He had taken notes while the Mayor was speaking and he proceeded to match victory with victory, defeat with defeat, anecdote with anecdote. 20 minutes, 25, 30 – some of the diners started fidgeting restlessly. A whisper was heard from one of the younger end, 'Isn't there going to be any dancing to-night?'

I was getting upset. Who would want to listen to me at this hour?

At last the Vice-chairman sat down and a sigh of relief, hidden under a round of applause, went through the party.

Now it would be my turn and I looked at the Chairman. He smiled and beckoned me to go to him.

'Billy, old chap. I wonder whether you would mind if I cancel your speech.'

I was flabbergasted: 'But why? I've got it ready.'

George pulled me a bit closer and whispered, 'There isn't time – those two have been far too long-winded.'

'But my speech only takes 13½ minutes,' I replied.

'That's all right,' said George, 'but there is old Ripley to reply to you, and he would keep us all night.'

From my conversation with Ripley I knew George was right, so I agreed.

As I sat down again beside Sally, George announced, 'Ladies and Gentlemen, the next item on the programme was to have been the proposal of the toast of the guests by our old friend Billy, but he has just asked me to be excused. This means that there will be no need for Mr. Ripley to reply. We shall miss Mr. Ripley's speech with regret; we hope that another opportunity to hear Mr. Ripley will arise in the not too distant future. This concludes the formal part of the evening and dancing will commence in a few minutes.'

Hearty applause greeted this announcement, but I could have wept with disappointment. Sally tried to console me by pointing out old Ripley's vexation, but my evening was spoilt.

A week later it was the club committee meeting again; I was still feeling sore and thinking about tendering my resignation. However, that was not necessary. George explained the whole business, thanked me profusely for collaborating to make the evening a success, and I was acclaimed the hero of the dinner.

My sacrifice had not been in vain and a special vote of thanks was recorded to me for the speech I never made.

# Life's Like That

When I arrived in Ghana to take a job as Surveyor for a tin mining company I knew nothing of the native language but I soon learnt one or two words. The most useful of these was 'Haka' which means 'thus' or 'likewise', and generally I found that the native 'boys' could understand what I wanted doing if I gave a demonstration and repeated the words 'Haka! haka!'

One day, however, I went with a party of 'boys' to survey a section of bush country. The ground was overgrown with vegetation and the 'boys' carried cutlasses to cut down the growth along the survey lines. Having got the first length cleared, I wanted to measure it and for this purpose used a surveyor's chain. This is a chain 66-feet long divided into 100 links and having a handle at each end. I held one end of the chain and tried by means of signs to tell one of the 'boys' to take the other end along the line, pull it taut and make a mark on the ground with his cutlass.

He took the end of the chain and pulled it taut but seemed to have no idea what to do next. So I took a nearby boy's cutlass and ran along the line, intending to demonstrate on the spot, shouting loudly, 'Haka! Haka! but, alas, he had misconstrued my intentions and all I saw was a pair of flying black legs which did not return for several days.

# The International Barber

Hearing a knock on the shop door, Bill looked up from the head of hair he was cutting and shouted, 'Come in and shut the door after you.' A tall, smartly dressed man made his way diffidently into the shop and asked quietly, 'Please, Mr. Barber, would you be willing to cut my hair?'

Bill looked at the stranger and smiled, 'Of course I will – provided that you have the money to pay me.'

'Then you don't mind that I am black man?'

Bill laughed: 'Not likely! I don't mind whether a man's black, yellow or green. If he's clean and has the money to pay, that is all I care. Chinese, Africans, Eskimos, they are just customers to me.'

The stranger sat in one of the vacant chairs and waited till Bill finished the other customers. Very soon they were suitably shorn and went off into the night with cheerful greetings to Bill who now turned to the negro, 'Will you sit in this chair, sir?'

A smile, and quickly the scissors were busy again – but not for long – the crinkly black hair was like wire and scissors were not tools for this job. Bill didn't worry – he connected up the electric shears and started a conversation.

The black man had suffered some unfortunate incidents and he expressed his pleasure that Bill had no racial prejudices. The old barber repeated his assertion that he did not mind whether his customers were Chinese, Africans or Eskimos and soon the tonsorial operation was completed satisfactorily.

Having paid Bill and added a substantial tip, the black man was about to depart into the night when he turned with a twinkle in his dark eyes and said, 'Tell me, Mr. Bill, do you have many Eskimos in your shop?'

# The Great White Chief

I hated him with all the feeling of which I was capable. George Bush, the exemplification of all those things which I desired for myself. He was a tall, upright man, a brilliant brain, good at sport, successful in business with a large car and a luxurious home and I worked for him.

What else could I do? I had very little experience – I couldn't get another job locally – I was just married and couldn't afford to move. I was cheap labour and George knew it.

I did everything to try to please him and he still grumbled or, what was worse, he laughed. I stayed late at the office so as to be there when he got back from visiting the jobs and my only reward was a curt, 'What – you still here, Norman?' He knew very well that I would be there – too frightened to go in case I was wanted. Then he would recount endless stories of his early adventures and expect me to laugh at his successes when all I wanted was to get home to my tea.

Yes, I hated him, but I daren't offend him – I could soon be replaced as he had no hesitation in reminding me from time to time.

Treatment of this kind could have only one of two results; either I would lose my identity entirely or I must have revenge. Revenge was my choice. What could I do? If only he could be made the laughing stock of the men instead of me.

I bided my time and then the opportunity for which I had been waiting came along. The firm were building a bridge over a river and the temporary timber supports for the bridge had been placed about half way across. It was quite risky walking along these timbers and, although I was used to it, I knew George was nervous of heights and kept away when he could. But one Friday afternoon he arrived on the job with the wages all made up in packets ready to hand out to the men. This was really my job but George liked to do it sometimes – personal contact he called it – no wonder he was nicknamed the Great White Chief. He came to the end of the scaffolding and called out, 'Norman!' I pretended not to hear – let him walk the plank. Out of the corner of my eye I saw him step gingerly on to the scaffold, obviously a bit scared but not going to show it if he could help it. He got halfway then called again, 'NORMAN COME HERE!'

This time everybody heard him and I dare not pretend deafness again – but I would show him. I strutted brightly along towards him, just to demonstrate how confident I was, then I stopped a bit short. 'Did you want me, sir?'

'Yes, you young idiot, I've been bawling my head off from the river bank. I've brought the wages, you can take them to the men.'

I stretched out my hand, then as he was about to give me the bag containing the wage packets, I pulled my hand back again. 'Sorry sir, I thought I was slipping.'

George was looking wild but not in the way I had expected. 'You ARE slipping, you fool. Hold on or you'll be in the river.'

It was too late. In my eagerness to show off and get my own back on George I had gone too far and in a matter of seconds I was in the water. I couldn't swim and thought 'this is the end.' I shut my eyes tight and went down in blackness. It was a surprise to come up again. I shouted and splashed but the water dragged me down again . . . then something grabbed hold of my collar and a familiar voice shouted, 'Be still, Norman, and you'll be all right.'

Yes, it was George and soon I was all right. He got pneumonia and I am running the office for a time but I shall be glad when he is back – I don't hate him any more.

Now, George is my 'Great White Chief' and I am his willing slave.